To

....

From

....

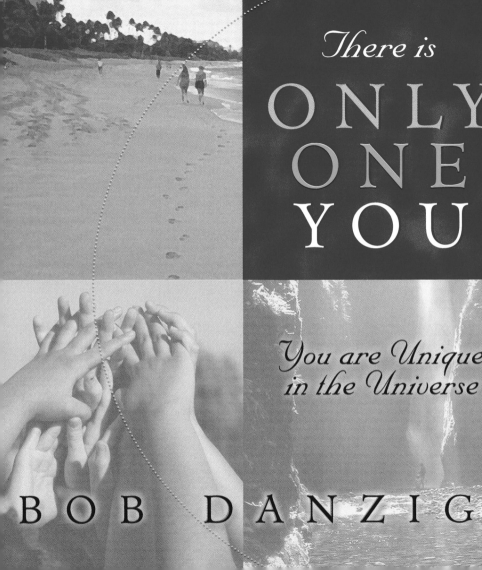

There is
ONLY
ONE
YOU

*You are Unique
in the Universe*

BOB DANZIG

CWLA Press is an imprint of the Child Welfare League of America. The Child Welfare League of America is the nation's oldest and largest membership-based child welfare organization. We are committed to engaging people everywhere in promoting the well-being of children, youth, and their families, and protecting every child from harm.

CHILD WELFARE LEAGUE OF AMERICA, INC.
HEADQUARTERS: 440 First Street, NW, Third Floor, Washington, DC 20001-2085
E-mail: books@cwla.org

CURRENT PRINTING
10 9 8 7 6 5 4 3 2 1

Cover and interior design by Tammy S. Grimes, 814.941.7447, www.tsgcrescent.com
'Comfort' image, Mother and Child by Pam Davidson, 973.674.2014, webdiva3@earthlink.net

Library of Congress Cataloging-in-Publication Data

Danzig, Robert J., 1932-
    There is only one you : you are unique in the universe / Bob Danzig.
        p. cm.
    ISBN 0-87868-884-6 (alk. paper)
    1. Individuality in children--Juvenile literature. [1. Individuality.] I. Title.
BF723.I56D36 2003
158.1--dc21
                                                                        2003003564
Printed in the United States of America .

Words are the seeds of our thought patterns. Words can influence our perspective, our horizon, our "self talk" and our destiny. My life was made more abundant when the social worker guiding me from my fourth to my fifth foster home told me, after every single meeting, "You are worthwhile." Those three words framed my mindset and never left me. It is my hope that some of the words you hear and read in this work will be etched in your own mindset and frame your sense of purpose and possibility.

B O B   D A N Z I G

To

PBD

To my bride, PBD, who has always managed to infuse into each of our five treasured children the sense that for each "There Is Only One You."

Thank you to my gifted book "babysitter," Callie Rucker Oettinger, who always seems to admonish with just the right touch—and result—and to the gifted spirit, imagination and fingers of Tammy Grimes, who brought unique design to every thought on every page—indeed "unique in the universe."

There is only one you!   You are unique in the universe

Only You Can

Hum your favorite song   March your favorite beat
Find your inner drummer   Follow your inner tune
Wink your eye   Blow your kiss
Ease your disappointment   Shed your tear
Smile your smile   Laugh your laugh   Have your heart
Celebrate your spirit
Share your voice   Choose your silence   Sing out loud
Take risks   Challenge limits   Welcome change
Explore your faith
Give your hug   Feel your joy
Be extraordinary!
Make your choices   Live your dreams

Remember your yesterday   Revel in your today
Explore your tomorrow
Share your gifts   Choose your attitude
Strengthen your confidence
Have your essence

You Deserve

Celebration   Admiration   Exhilaration
Love & Friendship   Courage & Strength
Champions
Harmony   Hope   Vision
Success   Purpose   Comfort
Appreciation & Respect   Serenity   Opportunity
Miracles
Tomorrow   Today   This moment   This second
Peace

Only you can

HUM Your Favorite Song

Hum Your Favorite Song

MARCH Your Favorite Beat

March Your Favorite Beat

FIND Your Inner Drummer

Find Your Inner Drummer

FOLLOW Your Inner Tune

Follow Your Inner Tune

Only You Can

Wink your Eye

Blow your Kiss

Only You Can

Ease your disappointment

Shed your fear

Only You Can

Smile *your smile*

Laugh *your laugh*

"Smiles generate smiles just as love generates love."

MOTHER TERESA

Only you can

Have your heart
Celebrate your spirit

Only You Can

share your voice

choose you

sing out loud

silence

Only You

Take Your Risks

Challenge Your Limits

Welcome Your Change

can

"Courage conquers all things."—Ovid

Only

"THE CENTRAL FACT IN THE LIVES
OF THE GREAT BELIEVERS IS THAT THEY
WENT FROM FAITH TO DOUBT. THEN
THEY BEGAN TO DOUBT THEIR DOUBTS."

–RABBI PHILIP LIPIS

EXPLORE

Only you

Can

GIVE YOUR

HUG

FEEL YOUR

JOY

Live your dreams

REMEMBER YOUR YESTERDAY

REVEL IN YOUR TODAY

EXPLORE YOUR TOMORROW

Only You Can

Share

your gifts

Only You can

choose
your
attitude

strengthen
your confidence

"Character and personal force are the only investments
that are worth anything." —WALT WHITMAN

Only You Can

HAVE

YOUR

ESSENCE

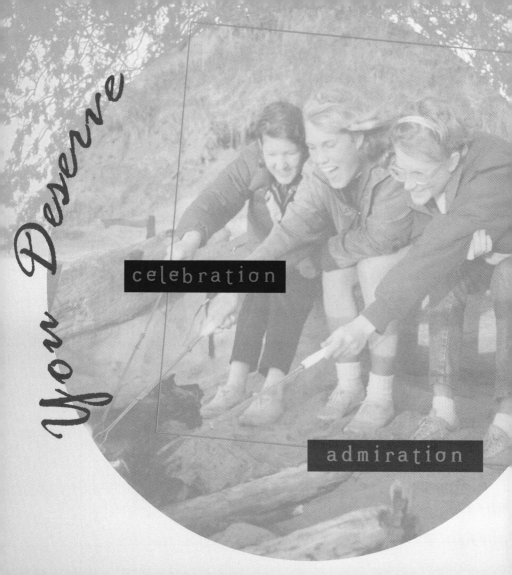

You Deserve

celebration

admiration

exhilaration

Love and

You Deserve

Friendship

you deserve

Courage *and* Strength

"Flowers grow out of dark moments."
—Corita Kent

CHAMPIONS
CHAMPIONS
CHAMPIONS
CHAMPIONS

You deserve
Harmony

You Deserve

Harmony

You
Deserve

Hope

Vision

"*I skate where the puck is going to be, not where it has been.*"

—WAYNE GRETZKY

you deserve

SUCCESS
PURPOSE

"THE SECRET OF SUCCESS IS CONSTANCY OF PURPOSE."

—BENJAMIN DISRAELI

You
deserve
Comfort

YOU DESERVE Appreciation & Respect

You deserve

SERENITY

You deserve

Opportunity

C L E S

"Miracles . . . seem to me to rest not so much upon faces or voices or healing power coming suddenly near us from far off, but upon our perceptions being made finer, so that for a moment our eyes can see and our ears can hear what is there about us always." —Willa Cather

You deserve

TODAY

TOMORROW

THIS MOMENT THIS SECOND

You Deserve

Peace

ABOUT THE AUTHOR

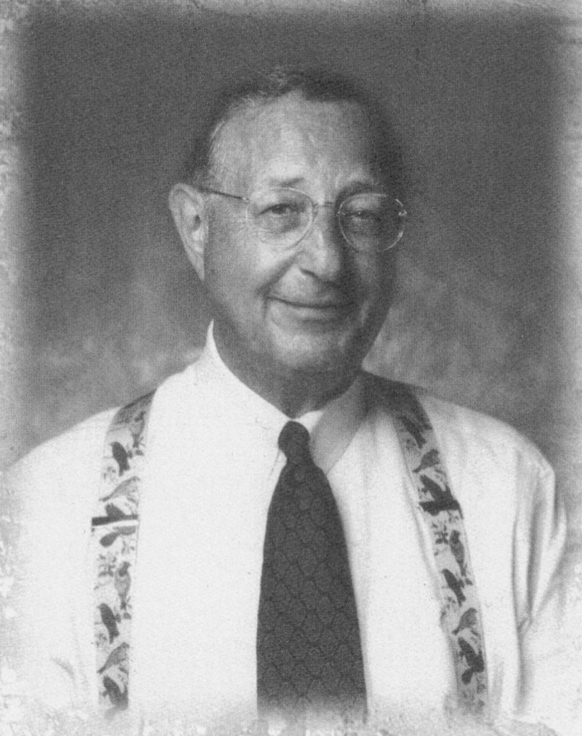

Bob Danzig grew from his five foster home background to office boy at his local newspaper, the Albany (N.Y.) *Times Union*, moved up the ladder to eventually become publisher of the same paper, and then on to two decades as CEO of the Hearst Newspaper Group and vice president of the Hearst Corporation. Now a published author and motivational speaker, he is also a member of the teaching faculty at the prestigious New School University and the leading hand guiding the Hearst Management Institute. His goal is to be an instrument for renewed affirmation that every single person is worthwhile. Bob's net speaking and author fees are donated to foster children (his passion) and gifted young musicians (his wife's passion).